This Book Belongs To

_____

Owen's CHOICE

The Night of the Halloween Vandals

Leah Butler and Trudy Peters
Illustrated by Neal Armstrong

SPENCER'S MILL PRESS
Charlotte, North Carolina

ISBN 0-9771666-0-0

Text and illustrations copyright ©2005 by Spencer's Mill Press
All rights reserved. Published by Spencer's Mill Press, LLC

Library of Congress Control Number: 2005906885

Printed in the U.S.A.
by Phoenix Color, Rockaway, N.J.

First printing September 2005

To children everywhere who are learning to make good choices,
and to Leona Peters, who helped bring this story to life

— L.B. and T.P.

ACKNOWLEDGEMENTS

The authors would like to thank Erica Stahler, our editor; as well as Janis McCarter, Leigh Hendry, Dina Stolpin, Penny Brooks, Natalie Cox Meade, Raye Dean Berry, Bob Brooks, Heather Dryden, Gary Seidler, Joe Pezzuto, Sam Gallucci, Albert and Kellie Buckley, and Camille Adcock.

The authors would also like to thank Leona Peters, Lucian Peters, Rae Hansberry, and George Hansberry, four remarkable parents who loved us through all of our choices!

NOTE FROM THE AUTHORS

Our goal is to teach children that every choice is important, not only in their own lives, but in the lives of everyone affected by the choices they make.

In each of our stories readers are allowed to make choices for the main character and consequently, through different story endings, experience the various outcomes of the wise or unwise choices they made.

Through the lives of the story characters our books give every parent and child, student and teacher, a sense of choices and consequences, as well as an even greater sense that courage, compassion, generosity, gratitude, and truth are essential to a responsible and rewarding life.

T. Winkle O'Toole

Spencer's Mill is about as small as a small town can be, and it sits right in the middle of nowhere. Very few people ever move to Spencer's Mill, and very few ever move away.

There are 583 adults and 422 kids who live here, along with one Irish firefly — me, T. Winkle O'Toole, but you can call me Wink.

I came to Spencer's Mill almost a year ago. Truth is, I hadn't planned on coming here at all. I was perfectly happy back home in Ireland with my friends and family. But then one day, on an adventure gone awry, I found myself trapped in a crate on a cargo ship bound for America.

I was a little confused when the crate opened in a strange, new place I'd never seen before. Then something magical began to happen. The air filled with a sweet smell more delicious than you can possibly imagine.

Turns out, there's a factory here in Spencer's Mill where pots bubble over with all sorts of incredible treats. The whole town smells of sweet caramel — it's everywhere!

Children are everywhere too. And sometimes the situations they get themselves into can be stickier than a pot full of caramel.

They could use some words of wisdom every now and then, but I can't talk to them like I can to you. Most of the time they don't even notice I'm around. So if you'd like to join me, together we can help them learn to make good choices.

There are lots of adventures to be had in Spencer's Mill. One thing's for sure, it's never boring! So, what do you say? Come on . . . let's get going!

When the sun falls out of the sky and the stars begin to twinkle, I head out for a night of adventure. Stretching my wings in the cool night air is what I live for. But it can be risky, too, especially when there are kids trying to catch me in jars with holes poked in the lids. Having a safe hiding spot is really a good idea if you're a firefly, so after a night of dodging jars, this old mailbox is one of my favorite places to hide out and rest.

I get in through the rusty hole, but it hasn't always been there. About a year ago some kids thought it would be fun to explode some firecrackers in here. The big boom made a small crack, then after a while the metal started to rust. Now there's a big hole.

The kids said they were "just having a little fun," but Ms. Hawkins called it vandalism. Now she'll have to buy a new mailbox — or start blow-drying her mail every time it rains.

Today there's a special letter in here for Owen. That's Ms. Hawkins's son; he's the new kid in town. Owen is still trying to make new friends — you know, figure out exactly where he fits in. He and his mom moved to Spencer's Mill a few months ago, right after Owen's grandmother died. She'd lived here all of her life and left her farm to Owen and his mom. Owen really likes living on the farm, but he doesn't like much of anything else about Spencer's Mill. Truth is, he hates it!

I bet this big orange envelope will put a smile on Owen's face. He should be here any minute. He's usually the last kid off the bus. There he is, the blond kid in the striped shirt.

"See you tomorrow, Mr. Hornsby," Owen said, jumping from the top step of the bus.

"Hey, Owen," called Mr. Hornsby, "do you like baseball?"

"Nah, not really," Owen said. "I play lacrosse. Well, at least I did before we moved here. Nobody's even heard of lacrosse in Spencer's Mill."

Mr. Hornsby ran his fingers through his hair, making it stand on end. Owen thought it looked funny, almost like he really did have horns.

"Well, most of the kids around here play baseball," Mr. Hornsby said. "Why don't you give it a try? It's fun. Who knows, you might even decide you like it."

"Maybe," Owen said, but he wasn't so sure. Nothing could be as much fun as lacrosse.

"Well, I'll see you in the morning, Owen," said Mr. Hornsby as he closed the bus door.

Owen wondered if anything would ever make Spencer's Mill fun. He emptied the rusted old mailbox, just like he did every day, and started up the long gravel drive. To his surprise, the envelope on the top of the stack was addressed to him.

Who would write to me? he thought.

The return address was Chadwick Drive. Owen had no idea where that was or who lived there. But just under *Chadwick Drive* he saw the words *Spencer's Mill*.

"Ugh . . . one thing's for sure, it can't be too exciting if it came from Spencer's Mill," he mumbled to himself.

The envelope was wrinkled and covered with drops of rain that had blown in through the rusty hole.

"Everything needs fixing around here," Owen said, whipping the soggy envelope across his leg. The ink smeared and rubbed off on his pants. "Oh, that's just great," he groaned, kicking a rock in disgust. He flipped the envelope over, tore open the flap, and pulled out a big, pumpkin-shaped invitation.

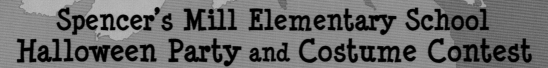

Spencer's Mill Elementary School
Halloween Party and Costume Contest

Friday, October 31
6:00 till 9:00 P.M.
in the school gym

Cast a secret ballot for the BEST COSTUME!

Pizza at 6:30
Trick-or-treating at 7:00
Ice cream, cookies, and games at 8:30

THE WINNING COSTUME
will be announced at the stroke of 9:00.
The winner will receive a year's supply of
Caramel Clump Clusters,
presented by the one and only
Miss Hildy Clump.

Owen's eyes lit up. Caramel Clump Clusters were his favorite candy. He'd been dying to meet Miss Hildy, too. Everyone said she was as old as the hills but acted just like a kid. They said she tasted every batch of candy before it left the factory, and all that sugar made her act a little crazy. She was so busy tasting she hardly ever left the factory. Owen just knew if he could win the costume contest, he wouldn't have to worry about fitting in and making new friends anymore. His new-kid troubles would be over!

Owen's mom had been one of the best costume designers in New York City before they moved to Spencer's Mill. His Halloween costumes had *always* been the best! He was pretty sure no one on Earth, and definitely no one in Spencer's Mill, could make a better costume than his mom.

Owen ran as fast as he could up the drive. As he burst through the door, he could barely catch his breath, much less speak.

"Mom! Mom, where are you?" he called out.

"Back here," his mom yelled from the spare bedroom she'd converted into her art studio.

Owen rushed in and shoved the invitation into her hand, almost knocking over a jar of purple-colored water filled with paintbrushes.

"Whoa, cowboy!" she said, grabbing the jar just before it teetered off the edge of her desk and crashed to the floor. "What's with all the excitement?"

"Mom, you gotta make me the greatest costume ever, the absolute best you've ever made!"

Owen's mom hadn't seen him this excited since they moved to Spencer's Mill. "This sounds like fun," she said, reading the invitation. "So, what do you want to be?" Ms. Hawkins had missed seeing the big smile that was now stretched across her son's face.

"I gotta think, I gotta think," Owen said, pacing back and forth. "It's gotta be the best one you've ever made — like nothing they've ever seen before!"

Owen headed for the kitchen to make his favorite afternoon snack, peanut butter and marshmallow toast. "I'll tell you as soon as I think of it," he said.

A hundred costumes came to Owen's mind, but not the right one. Too easy . . . not good enough . . . not scary enough. They had only a week, so he had to think fast!

"Hey, Owen, your dad called today," his mom yelled. "He wants you to come over after school next Friday to help Amy and Joey carve pumpkins. Would you like to do that?"

"Sure, no problem," Owen answered. "And after that I can just walk over to the Halloween party. It's only a block away."

Owen really liked going to his dad's house. He actually used to live in Spencer's Mill a long time ago, he was just too young to remember. He was only two years old when his mom and dad got divorced. That's when Owen and his mom left Spencer's Mill and moved to New York City. His dad, Mr. Hawkins, had stayed in Spencer's Mill and gotten married again. Now Owen had a little stepsister and stepbrother named Amy and Joey. He was the big brother when he went to his dad's house, and he especially liked that.

Owen peeked inside the toaster oven. He loved watching the marshmallows and peanut butter melt into a gooey glob on top of the toast. His stomach growled. All this thinking was making him hungry. His costume would have to be one-of-a-kind. If it was totally awesome, then maybe Nick and Eddie would ask him to trick-or-treat with them. They were the coolest guys in the whole third grade. It seemed like they were always having fun.

Living in Spencer's Mill wouldn't be so bad if I had some cool friends, Owen thought. *I might even try playing baseball.*

Owen looked out the kitchen window at the little white house just up the road. Todd, a fifth grader, lived there. Owen sometimes sat in his bedroom window and watched Todd and his dad pitching balls after supper.

This was Todd's last year at Spencer's Mill Elementary, so he'd definitely be at the Halloween party. If Owen could win the contest, maybe Todd would want to pitch balls with him.

Suddenly it came to him. "Mom, I've got it!" he yelled. "How 'bout a swamp creature?" He grabbed his sticky snack from the toaster oven and ran back to her studio.

"You know," he said, making his best scary face, "something really creepy and totally gross!"

"Sounds good to me," she said, making her own scary face right back at Owen. "If it's a swamp creature, it should definitely have some snakes. And how about a long black cape?" she added.

"Yeah! And can you make it moan and groan, too?" he asked, laughing.

"You're really going to put me to work, aren't you?" she said, laughing along with Owen. "I'll give it my best shot, boss man — I mean, Swamp Man."

The next week was spent working on Owen's costume. First they sketched a design, then they gathered all the materials so Ms. Hawkins could make the costume. By Halloween it was finally finished, complete with a tape recorder sewn inside the cape that played creepy moaning and groaning sounds when Owen pressed a small button. And for the final touch Ms. Hawkins added two battery-operated glowing eyeballs.

After school on Friday, Owen tried on his costume. The tape recorder worked perfectly. He was so excited he could hardly wait for the party, but first he would have a chance to try out his costume on Amy and Joey!

Amy and Joey were waiting on the porch, sitting on top of two big orange pumpkins, when Owen and his mom pulled up.

"Thanks for the ride, Mom," Owen said as he grabbed the brown paper bag containing his costume.

"Glad to be at your service, Swamp Man," she said. "I'll pick you up at nine o'clock in front of the gym, okay?"

"Yep, sounds good," Owen said.

Ms. Hawkins waved to Amy and Joey, then drove away just as Amy ran down the walk and wrapped her arms around Owen's leg. Owen dropped his bag, swooped her up over his head, and spun her around in a circle. She loved that.

"We got pumpkins for jack-o'-wanterns!" said Amy, bouncing up and down.

"I think you mean 'lanterns,'" said Owen.

Amy scrunched her eyebrows together. "That's what I said!"

Owen gently put her down, then quickly grabbed the brown paper bag just as Joey started to peek inside.

"Later, buddy. It's a surprise," Owen said with a wink. Joey grinned from ear to ear. He really liked surprises.

Joey picked up the largest pumpkin to show Owen how strong he was. He wobbled backward, trying to keep his balance.

"Wow, Joey! How'd you lift that?" Owen said, rescuing the pumpkin just as it started to roll out of Joey's arms. "It's almost too heavy for me."

Joey beamed thinking about how strong he looked. That made Amy want to pick hers up too. She tried to lift the other one, but it wouldn't budge. "This is my jack-o'-wantern," she said, pointing to the smaller one.

"And it's a fine jack-o'-*wantern* too," Owen said. "We're going to make it reeeeeally scary."

It seemed like it took Owen forever to trace scary goblin faces onto the front of each pumpkin. Amy and Joey were beginning to fidget in their seats by the time he was ready to start carving.

Long before he was finished, Owen's hands were aching and he was wearing two of Amy's cartoon-covered bandages. He'd managed to poke himself a couple of times with the end of the carving tool.

"Done!" Owen finally said. The jack-o'-lanterns looked great! But the real test was how they'd look in the dark. Owen and his dad took the lanterns into a bathroom with no windows. Amy and Joey followed close behind, giggling with excitement. Mr. Hawkins centered a small white candle in the belly of each pumpkin and then lit them. With the flip of a switch the room was pitch black. Amy screamed with delight as a bright orange glow flickered inside the pumpkins.

"I'm going to keep mine forever and ever," Amy said, once again wrapping her arms around Owen's leg. Amy was big on saying "forever and ever."

"Good job, son," Mr. Hawkins said with a smile. "And lots of hard work, too . . . I really appreciate it."

"No sweat," said Owen, feeling pretty proud of himself. He liked doing things that made people happy. His dad was happy, Amy and Joey were happy, and come to think of it . . . he was too!

"Hey, Dad, remember a few weeks ago when you asked if I wanted a baseball glove and I said no?"

"Sure do. Have you changed your mind?"

"Well, most of the kids around here like to play baseball, so I thought I might give it a try."

"I think that's a great idea," his dad answered. How 'bout we go for breakfast at Long's Grill in the morning, then after we eat, we'll walk next door to Reed's Hardware and pick out a glove?"

"That'd be great. Can we get some of their blueberry pancakes?" asked Owen. Without a doubt, Long's blueberry pancakes were his very favorite.

"Sounds good to me. It's a plan, man!" Mr. Hawkins said, laughing. Owen laughed too. He liked it when his dad tried to be funny.

Owen changed into his costume while Amy and Joey finished their dinner, then he reappeared, stomping across the room as Swamp Man. He stopped in front of Amy's chair and pushed the button inside his cape. When Amy heard the creepy moaning and groaning sounds, her eyes grew as big as saucers. She screamed, jumped down from her chair, and in all the confusion, lost her balance and plopped to the floor with a *thump!*

"It's okay, Amy. It's just me," Owen said, quickly pulling off his mask. He showed Amy the tape recorder and let her press the button a few times. Judging from Amy's reaction, his costume was a huge success. But would everyone at the party be as impressed? Owen sure hoped so.

Owen arrived at the party a few minutes late, hoping everyone would already be there when Swamp Man showed up in full costume. The front of the gym was covered with Halloween decorations. Orange and black helium balloons lined the sidewalk. They were gathered in bunches and tied to bricks so they wouldn't float away.

Owen took a deep breath and pushed open the heavy gymnasium doors. A hush filled the room when he stepped inside. It was like someone had turned down the volume.

Everyone turned to look at the creepy creature that had just walked through the doors.

"Who is that?" "*What* is that!" they whispered back and forth. No one knew. Finally Owen lifted his mask, revealing his true identity.

The room buzzed with questions about his costume: Where had it come from? Who had made it? Did he order it? Did it come in different sizes? Most of the kids wanted to know if they could borrow it for next Halloween.

Ah, success. Sweet success! Owen couldn't have been more thrilled!

I know what you're thinking . . . things are looking pretty good for Owen, right? But things aren't always as they seem. The night is young, and this adventure has just begun. The costume contest is only the first of many challenges Owen will face on this Halloween night.

The ballots had been cast and only a few scraps of pizza were left on the tables when kids started gathering into groups.

"Hey, Swamp Man, wanna come with us?" It was Nick and Eddie, the boys Owen wanted to trick-or-treat with.

His costume had worked!

"Okay, sure," Owen said. Spencer's Mill was getting better by the minute.

The three boys headed for the exits at the front of the gym, where two other costumed friends of Nick and Eddie's were waiting outside to join them.

Owen glanced around the room, hoping he was still the center of attention. His eyes landed on Todd, the fifth grader who lived in the white house up the road from him. Todd had on a long black cape that swept the floor as he walked. The white fangs and the blood leaking from the corners of his mouth were a dead giveaway for Count Dracula.

"Hey, Todd. Cool costume," Owen said.

"Thanks, but yours is definitely gonna win," Todd said. "If you don't have anyone to trick-or-treat with, you can come with us." Then Todd pointed to a group of older kids standing behind him.

Owen wasn't sure what to say. He really wanted to get to know Todd, but Nick was waving for him to come.

"I just told some other guys I'd go with them," Owen answered, "but maybe I'll see you later."

"Okay," Todd said, looking over at Nick and Eddie. It was obvious Owen's new friends were in a big hurry.

As the boys walked out of the gym, Eddie took a paper clip out of his pocket and — *pop! pow!* — two shriveled balloons dropped to the ground.

Nick led the boys past the first street they came to. He seemed to know exactly where he was going.

What's wrong with that street? Owen wondered. *Don't those houses have candy too?* It seemed a little strange to skip a street, but Owen wasn't about to ask questions. He was trick-or-treating with the cool guys, and that's all that mattered.

When Nick came to the second street, he made a quick turn and the other boys followed. It was Owen's dad's street. Just after they rounded the corner, Nick turned and gave everyone the signal to stop.

"All right, we're going to do it again this year. Right, guys?" he said.

"Yeah, yeah," the other boys chimed in. Owen could feel their excitement.

"Do what?" Owen asked curiously.

"Smash pumpkins, what else?" Nick said.

"You mean jack-o'-lanterns?"

Nick was annoyed by Owen's question. "What other kind of pumpkins are there on Halloween? It's more fun than trick-or-treating, anytime. Right, guys?" said Nick. "And were gonna get Ol' Man Drake's this year too," he added. "That'll teach him not to yell at us when we cut through his yard."

Owen looked at the others. They were all nodding.

"Uh, are you sure?" Owen said. He knew Mr. Drake was really grumpy and always yelling at the kids who cut through his yard, but . . .

Bzzzzz . . . bzzzzz. A small bug started to buzz around Nick's head.

"What's up with this bug?" Nick said, slapping at his ear.

"I don't know. Maybe we're standing too close to its nest or something," Eddie answered.

Owen hadn't noticed a thing. He just stood there frozen. Lucky for him, the bug was keeping the boys distracted while he tried to decide what to do.

Finally Nick turned to Owen in disgust. "Stop thinking so much! They're just pumpkins. They'll get thrown out tomorrow anyway."

Not Amy's, Owen thought. *She's going to keep hers "forever and ever"!*

"You're not afraid, are you, Swaaaamp Man?" Eddie teased, swatting at the bug, which was still zipping back and forth.

"No, I'm not afraid. It's just that . . . well, I thought —"

Before Owen could finish his sentence, Nick interrupted, "Even if someone sees us, they won't recognize us in our costumes."

"Yeah, and they're just big orange vegetables!" laughed Eddie. "Even if we get caught, you can't go to jail for smashing *vegetables*!"

"We're not gonna get caught," Nick said. "We didn't get caught last year, and we won't get caught this year either. So let's get going before someone catches up with us. Besides, this bug is driving me crazy!"

Owen's brain was racing at warp speed. Eddie was right; jack-o'-lanterns were just vegetables. They'd be thrown out tomorrow — all but Amy's, that is. But what about all the other kids who'd worked really hard on their pumpkins? If Owen went along, he could make sure the boys skipped his dad's house, so at least Amy's and Joey's pumpkins wouldn't get smashed. That was a good reason to go, he thought. Besides, just going along didn't mean he'd have to smash anything. And if Ol' Man Drake's pumpkin *did* get smashed, maybe he'd learn a lesson and stop yelling at everyone who cut through his yard. Most of all, Owen just wanted to fit in. He knew if Nick, Eddie, and the other guys thought he was scared, they'd make fun of him for the rest of the year. Then no one would want to be his friend.

But what if they did get caught? His mom would be really disappointed in him, especially after she had worked so hard on his costume. But his costume was black as night; no one would see him. And if they did get caught, he could explain to his mom and dad that he'd only gone along to save Amy's and Joey's pumpkins. But Nick had said they wouldn't get caught, so he didn't need to worry about that. It was almost too much to think about!

Ahhh, things aren't always as they seem.
Owen has a tough choice to make.
What should he do?
You can help him choose.

 Owen should not go with Nick and Eddie, even if it means that they will make fun of him and that Amy's and Joey's pumpkins will get smashed.

 Owen should go with Nick and Eddie to make sure Amy's and Joey's pumpkins don't get smashed, but he should not smash any pumpkins himself, even if Nick and Eddie tease him and call him names.

 Owen should go with Nick and Eddie. He can save Amy's and Joey's pumpkins, and if he has to smash one himself to keep Nick and Eddie from calling him names, he can smash Ol' Man Drake's. It might even teach Ol' Man Drake a lesson.

"So, what's it gonna be, Swamp Man?" asked Nick. "Are you comin' or not?"

It just didn't seem right to Owen, too many things could go wrong.

"You know," Owen answered, "a lot of kids are gonna be really upset when they see their pumpkins splattered all over the place." Owen looked over his shoulder and saw other groups of trick-or-treaters turning down the street Nick had just passed by. He wished he could be with them instead of Nick and Eddie.

"What are you — chicken?" one of the boys teased.

"No, I just don't like messin' with other people's stuff," Owen said. "Haven't you ever carved a jack-o'-lantern you were really proud of?" he asked.

A kid dressed like Frankenstein stepped forward.

"Maybe Owen's right," he said. "I don't want anyone messin' with my pumpkin. It's the best one I've ever carved, and it took me forever!" he added.

The other boys just looked at one another.

"Looks like Swamp Man and Frankenstein are *both* chicken," Nick said. "Come on, guys, we're wasting time." With that, the other boys walked away, leaving Owen and Frankenstein behind.

The lonesome pair backtracked to the school in silence. They both knew they'd be targets for Nick and Eddie's jokes come Monday morning, and probably for the rest of the year.

No sooner were they back at the school than Frankenstein spotted a friend and ran off, leaving Owen all by himself.

"That's just great," Owen said, looking around. "I guess I'll be trick-or-treating with me, me, and oh yeah . . . *me*!" Trick-or-treating alone would not be good; it wasn't natural for a normal kid. Actually, it was really *weird*!

Owen was certain the gym would be empty by now. He thought about going back inside and waiting for everyone to return. That would be an almost normal thing to do, and almost normal was definitely better than *totally weird!*

As he made his way back up the sidewalk to the gym, he was surprised to see a group of kids just leaving.

"Thank goodness," Owen whispered to himself. He was even more relieved when he recognized one of the costumes. It was Count Dracula.

"Hey, Todd," Owen yelled, "I changed my mind. Is it okay if I come with you guys?"

"Let me guess," said Todd, "Nick and Eddie wanted to smash pumpkins, right?"

"How'd you know?" Owen asked.

"All the kids know," Todd answered. "They did it last year too, they just didn't get caught."

Owen wished he'd known. He wondered how he could've been so wrong about Nick and Eddie.

This time Count Dracula, Swamp Man, and the other trick-or-treaters turned down the street that Nick had passed by. They zigzagged back and forth down the street, making sure to knock on every single door.

Their bags were already plump with candy by the time they reached the end of the block. When Owen looked in both directions before crossing the street, he caught sight of Nick, Eddie, and the others just one block over. A jack-o'-lantern lay in bits at their feet.

They've probably already smashed Amy's and Joey's, Owen thought. A knot grew tight in his stomach, making the ball of candy in his mouth taste sour. He imagined how disappointed Amy and Joey would be in the morning. Especially Amy. Her pumpkin hadn't made it *four hours,* much less *forever!*

By the time they got back to the gym, Owen's arms felt weak and his fingers had red marks across them. His candy bag was heavy enough to sink a ship!

Nick and Eddie and the other boys had already gathered in the corner. Owen figured they'd probably sniffed out and destroyed every last pumpkin in Spencer's Mill.

"Attention! Attention, everyone!" It was Miss Hildy. Owen stood on his tiptoes to get a better look. She was barely as tall as he was. She had rosy red cheeks and golden brown hair that was piled on top of her head and held in place by what looked like a stick of candy.

"It's nine o'clock," Miss Hildy said, giggling into the microphone, "and we all know what that means."

Owen held his breath and crossed his fingers behind his back. He wanted this more than anything!

Miss Hildy gently opened the envelope and announced into the microphone, "The winner of this year's contest is . . . Owen Hawkins, better known as Swamp Man!"

He'd done it! He'd actually won!

"Well, don't just stand there," Todd said, poking Owen in the ribs. "Get movin'."

Everyone cheered as Owen walked to the front of the gym to meet Miss Hildy and collect his prize.

Miss Hildy handed Owen a shiny red box. "This box is very special, Owen Hawkins," she said, "not only because it contains some of our most scrumptious candy, but also . . . "— she leaned in a little closer — "whenever it's empty, you can bring it to the factory and I'll fill it up again." Owen liked the sound of her voice, and he couldn't help but notice she smelled just like caramel apples. "And it's yours for one year," she added.

"Thank you, ma'am," he said, tucking the box under his arm. "I'll take real good care of it."

Moments later Owen was back in the crowd celebrating with Todd and his friends. Others came over to join in, and before long Owen was making new friends of his own. His costume had worked!

When the party was over, he ran down the sidewalk to his mom's car.

"I did it, Mom! I mean *we* did it!" he said, jumping into the backseat.

"Well, what'd you expect?" she laughed. "You asked for a winning costume, and that's what I gave you!"

"Now, let's not forget our deal," she said, stretching her arm over the seat. "Hand 'em over, buddy!" They both knew she had a monster sweet tooth and could smell a Caramel Clump Cluster a mile away.

"Miss Hildy will keep it filled for a whole year, Mom," Owen said, placing the shiny red box in the palm of her hand. "As much as we can eat!"

He still couldn't believe it. "For a *whole* year!"

Owen was too excited to sleep when he got home. He turned his candy bag upside down over his bed so he could pick out his favorite pieces.

Finally Owen climbed under the covers and turned out the light. He barely noticed the full autumn moon shining through his window. He was thinking about Amy and Joey and how they would find their pumpkins splattered all over the walk first thing in the morning. Owen knew how upset they'd be. He wondered if there was anything he could have done to keep their pumpkins from getting smashed.

The next morning, up to his elbows in sticky syrup and blueberry pancakes, Owen told his dad all about winning the contest and meeting Miss Hildy.

"We had an interesting night ourselves," Mr. Hawkins said, pushing a bite of pancake through the pool of syrup on his plate. "I hate to tell you this, son, but someone smashed Amy's and Joey's pumpkins last night."

Owen took a big gulp of cold milk, giving himself a few seconds to decide if he should tell his dad what he knew.

"Uh . . . Dad," he said, hesitating. "About Amy's and Joey's pumpkins . . . I think I know who did it."

"What do you mean, Owen?" his dad asked.

"I was gonna trick-or-treat with the guys who smashed their pumpkins. But I didn't know that's what they were gonna do. I mean, when I found out, I decided not to go with them." Owen's pancakes didn't taste so great anymore. "We were headed down your street, and I knew Amy's and Joey's pumpkins were gonna get smashed. So I tried to talk them out of it." Owen wasn't sure he was making sense. He was a little confused himself.

"So let me get this straight, Owen. The boys you were with wanted to smash pumpkins, and you tried to talk them out of it? Is that right?"

"Yes," Owen answered. "But if I'd gone along, I could've saved Amy's and Joey's pumpkins."

"No, you did the right thing, Owen. It takes a brave person to stand up for what he believes in. Most grown-ups would have a hard time doing what you did last night."

"But what about Amy and Joey?" Owen asked. "Their pumpkins got demolished!"

"Yes, they were upset, especially Amy. She was outside early this morning trying to put her jack-o'-lantern back together," Mr. Hawkins answered.

"But it wasn't your fault, Owen," he added. "You had nothing to do with it.

You made the right choice by not going with those boys. They might have made a different choice too if they'd seen how upset little kids like Amy were this morning. But Amy will recover. She may not have her jack-o'-lantern 'forever and ever,' but she'll always have a big brother to help her make good choices.

"You know, son, there's a word for what those boys did last night. It's called vandalism. There are lots of ways to have fun, but destroying something that doesn't belong to you is *not* one of them." Mr. Hawkins looked into Owen's eyes. "Respecting other people's property helps us all live together peacefully. Unfortunately, some folks don't understand that."

"Like the guys last night?" asked Owen.

"That's right," Mr. Hawkins answered. "I know it's hard to make friends when you're the new kid, but always choose your friends carefully, son. Remember, your friends will help shape who you become someday. They should be kids you admire and want to be like."

Owen thought of Todd. He'd like to be like Todd.

"Cuckoo! Cuckoo!" A little red bird popped out of an old wooden clock hanging on the wall.

"Hey, Dad, it's ten o'clock! Time for Reed's to open!"

This was Owen's first time in Reed's Hardware. It smelled like leather and fresh sawdust. The wooden floors were lopsided and worn in spots, creaking when Owen walked on them.

It didn't take long to spot Mr. Reed, wearing a New York Yankees baseball cap. Owen had heard he was a big baseball fan.

"I hope we'll be seeing you on the Spencer's Mill baseball field, young man!" said Mr. Reed as he dropped Owen's new glove into a paper bag. "You know, in a few years, if you're on the team that wins the fifth-grade championship, you'll get to come fishing at my cabin on the lake. The fish are so big they jump right in your boat!" Mr. Reed added with a wink.

"Wow, that'd be great!" Owen tried to imagine a fish jumping into a boat.

On the way home he started to think more about baseball and fishing at Mr. Reed's cabin. Maybe, just maybe, Spencer's Mill was going to be a good place to live after all.

Turns out Owen made a good choice last night.
Next time you're in a fix, ask yourself what feels right.
You can make good choices just like Owen.
Until we meet again, keep the twinkle in your eye,
the wind in your wings, and the goodness in your heart!

"So, what's it gonna be, Swamp Man?" asked Nick. "Are you comin' or not?" Nick wanted to get going.

"Uh, sure . . . why not?" answered Owen.

His plan was to protect Amy's and Joey's pumpkins. *That's all I have to do,* he told himself. But what if they asked him to smash a pumpkin? What would his plan be then? There hadn't been time for Owen to think about that. It was starting to feel a little warm inside his costume.

The boys headed down the street, ducking behind bushes and trash cans, searching for an easy target. The first house they came to didn't have a pumpkin, and the second house had only a glowing plastic witch hanging from a nail on the front door.

"It's their lucky night," Owen mumbled to himself.

"What'd you say, Owen?" asked Eddie.

"I said . . . I'm glad it's not a *yucky* night. You know . . . no rain."

Eddie leaned over and whispered in Nick's ear, "This new kid's a little weird."

"Hey, guys, check this out!" yelled one of the boys, who was dressed like Frankenstein. Everyone ran and joined him, squatting behind a hedgerow of holly bushes. One at a time they poked their heads over the top. Just on the other side sat two perfectly carved pumpkins — Amy's and Joey's! Owen sank to his knees. He couldn't believe it had come to this already.

"All right, men, who's goin' first?" Nick rubbed his hands together, hungry for action.

"Uhhhh . . . ," moaned Owen. He had a huge lump in his throat, and the heat inside his costume was rising.

"Go ahead, Owen," Nick said. "They're all yours!" He tried to give Owen a high five, but Owen didn't even notice. His eyes were still fixed on Amy's and Joey's pumpkins.

"A-a-actually, this house happens to be m-my dad's," stuttered Owen.

"Yeah, so?" said Nick.

"So, we spent all afternoon carving those pumpkins." Owen tried to swallow. "Can't we just skip these two?" Behind his mask a bead of sweat rolled down his forehead.

The boys looked at one another, then at the goblin-faced pumpkins, then back at Nick.

"All right," Nick said, "let's keep moving. There're more pumpkins where these came from."

Nick was right, there were a *lot* more! And Owen went along, watching as the other boys splattered pumpkin after pumpkin on the ground.

"Hey, Owen, you haven't had a turn yet," Nick said, tossing a small pumpkin into the air. It splintered over a fence post and fell to the ground in chunks.

"Hey, there's Ol' Man Drake's place!" Eddie said, pointing to the house on the next corner. "How 'bout that one, Owen?"

"Yeah . . . good one," the others agreed. "Go for it, Owen!"

The boys ran ahead, eagerly waving for Owen to catch up.

"It's all yours, Swamp Man," Eddie said, holding the heavy iron gate open for Owen to pass through.

"Nah," said Owen. "Thanks anyway." He took a tiny step backward, remembering his plan.

"What are you, chicken or something?" teased Nick.

"Come on, Swamp Man, it's fun," another boy added, trying to encourage Owen.

"Yeah, go ahead, chicken!" said Eddie.

"Aw, he's a scaredy-cat."

Owen looked at the pumpkin sitting beside Mr. Drake's front door. It was squatty and a little lopsided, too. Definitely not the best carving job Owen had ever seen.

"So, what are you afraid of, Swamp Man?" asked Eddie.

Owen wished they'd stop making fun of him. He wanted to cover his ears and make them go away.

"Good grief!" groaned Nick. "What's the big deal?"

Tired of waiting, Nick ran up the walk, grabbed the pumpkin, and threw it to the ground at Owen's feet.

"See, Swamp Chicken?" he shouted. "There's nothing to it!"

Owen looked down at the broken pumpkin. A small white candle rolled off the sidewalk and into the gutter. A thin line of smoke floated through the air. He could feel the others looking at him as he stood there speechless. Someone else was looking at him too, someone Owen hadn't expected.

When Owen looked up, he was staring straight at Count Dracula! Todd and his friends were crossing the street just one block over, the same street Owen's group had just passed by. Owen quickly looked away.

Who am I kidding? he thought. *I'm a dead giveaway in this costume!*

He wanted to hide behind someone or something. But he was standing there all alone. The smashers had run off and abandoned him. They'd finally figured out Owen didn't have what it took to be one of them.

Owen could think of only one thing: Todd thought he did have what it took to be a smasher.

Owen ran back to the gym as fast as he could. He was embarrassed to go back inside alone, so he hid in the bushes and waited till he could sneak in behind some other kids.

The gym was exploding with noise and excitement. Kids were trading candy and comparing the size of their bags. Owen's bag was completely empty. He rolled it up and stuffed it down the back of his pants, hoping no one would notice.

Nick, Eddie, and the others were the last group back to the gym. They huddled in the corner, whispering and pointing in Owen's direction. Todd and his group were laughing and having fun at the other end of the gym. Owen wished he had someone to be with. He wasn't sure where he belonged — or even *if* he belonged.

"Testing . . . one, two, three. Testing."

It was Miss Hildy. She was standing on a chair, microphone in one hand and the grand prize in the other.

Somehow, winning the contest didn't seem so important to Owen anymore. Just getting through the rest of the party would be challenge enough.

Miss Hildy gently tore open a gold-colored envelope and spoke into the microphone again. "I am so thrilled to have been chosen to announce this year's winner for Best Costume," she said, giggling. Slowly she pulled a white piece of paper from the envelope and wiggled her tiny glasses to the end of her nose.

"And the winner of this year's contest is . . . Owen Hawkins, the Swamp Man!"

Owen's stomach did a somersault.

Everyone clapped and cheered as he walked to the front of the gym to accept his prize. Everyone, that is, except a few boys huddled in the corner.

"Ol' Swamp Man's not as big and bad as he seems," Nick yelled.

"Yeah, he's probably afraid of the swamp," Eddie added.

Owen cringed. This was the moment he had been dreading. And the entire elementary school was there to witness his downfall! It wasn't until after he'd collected his prize and was standing there searching for the nearest exit that he realized everyone was still clapping. No one seemed to be paying attention to Nick and Eddie. Quite the opposite; everyone was ignoring them.

"Hey, Owen," Todd said, "I knew you'd win."

"Thanks," Owen replied, feeling uncomfortable and ashamed. He could barely look at Todd.

"Okay, trick-or-treaters," Miss Hildy said, tapping the microphone. "It's time for everyone to go home. All of you have a fun weekend!"

The noisy gym emptied quickly as kids funneled out through two sets of double doors.

"Hey, what happened to all the balloons?" one kid asked.

Todd leaned over and whispered to Owen, "I bet Nick and Eddie popped them."

"How'd you know?" Owen asked, feeling embarrassed that he'd been with them when it happened.

"They did it last year — and smashed a bunch of pumpkins, too," said Todd.

"Umm . . . about the pumpkins . . ." Owen knew this was his chance to explain. "I didn't smash any."

"Why not?"

"I don't know, I guess I just didn't feel like it. I only went along to keep my brother's and sister's pumpkins from getting smashed, but then —"

"They ditched you, right?" Todd interrupted.

"Yeah, how'd you know?" Owen asked.

"I saw you walking back to the gym by yourself," Todd said. "Look . . . just forget about it, Owen. They're not the kind of kids you want to be friends with anyway."

"Yeah, I guess I figured that out the hard way," Owen said.

As soon as he got in his mom's car, Owen told her all about winning the contest, but after that he barely uttered a sound. Ms. Hawkins assumed he was exhausted from all the excitement, but Owen just wanted to put this night behind him and wake up to a brand-new day — one that didn't include smashing pumpkins.

Owen had his costume off and one foot in bed when he noticed the clumps of dried-up pumpkin seeds stuck to the bottom of his cape. He sat down in the middle of the floor and went to work. For each seed he pulled off, he remembered a pumpkin that had been smashed. He knew he'd never forget this Halloween, and not because he'd won the contest. This would always be the Halloween with *no* friends, *no* fun, and *no* trick-or-treating!

Owen did manage to save Amy's and Joey's pumpkins, but what about all the fun he could have had trick-or-treating? Do you think it might have made a difference if he'd told the smashers how he felt about vandalism?

The next morning Owen climbed into the seat of his dad's truck.

"So, did you win?" Mr. Hawkins asked.

"Yes," Owen answered.

"That's it? Just 'yes'? You don't seem very excited." Mr. Hawkins had expected a little more enthusiasm. "Who did you trick-or-treat with?" he asked, hoping to hear more about Owen's big night.

"Just some guys," Owen answered, wishing his dad would talk about something else.

"We looked for you last night. Did you and your friends come through the neighborhood?"

Owen didn't answer. He just sat there in a daze, imagining folks going out to get their morning newspaper and finding a mess of splattered pumpkins instead. It would be the news, all right, just not the news they were expecting.

"Owen . . . uh, son? Did a witch cast a spell on you last night?"

"Huh?" Owen said, looking over at his dad.

"Are you okay?" Mr. Hawkins asked, pulling up to the curb in front of Long's Grill. He parked the truck and turned in his seat to face Owen. "Is something wrong, son?"

"Kinda," Owen answered slowly. "The kids I was with last night . . . well, they smashed a bunch of pumpkins."

Mr. Hawkins raised his eyebrows. "I saw the mess this morning, up and down both sides of the street. There was enough smashed pumpkin to make twenty pies." The tone in Mr. Hawkins's voice suddenly sounded more serious. "Did you have anything to do with it, Owen?"

"No, that's the good news . . . and the bad news." Owen hung his head. "I went so I could keep Amy's and Joey's pumpkins from getting smashed, which I did, but when it was my turn, I didn't want to do it. They all laughed at me, Dad.

It was a lousy night. And now I feel awful even though I didn't do anything."

"Well, son," Mr. Hawkins said, putting his hand on Owen's shoulder. "Sounds like you were trying to do the right thing but ended up with some boys who were doing the wrong thing. Does that sound about right?"

"Yeah, I guess so." Owen wasn't quite sure.

"When other kids want you to do something that makes you feel uncomfortable or just doesn't feel right, all you have to do is come home. When you go along like you did last night, it only makes you feel bad, and it can get you in trouble, too. No one should destroy another person's property. It's called vandalism. Maybe it would have made a difference if you had told the boys how you felt, or maybe not, but at least you could have walked away knowing you did the right thing, and that's what counts."

"But what about Amy's and Joey's pumpkins?" Owen asked.

"You're right, Amy and Joey would've been upset," answered Mr. Hawkins, "but only for a day or two, and then it would've been forgotten. Another thing to remember . . . ," added Mr. Hawkins, "when you go along with kids who are doing something wrong, it makes *you* look guilty too, just being with them."

"Do you mean guilty by association?" Owen asked. He'd heard that before.

"That's right. As the saying goes — we're known by the company we keep. That means people will think you're just like the kids you're with."

Owen thought about how it had looked when Todd saw him with Nick and Eddie. If he hadn't had a chance to explain, Todd would probably think he was a smasher.

"I think you learned a valuable lesson last night," said Mr. Hawkins, ruffling Owen's hair. "Sometimes we learn our lessons the easy way, and sometimes we learn 'em the hard way." Owen could tell his dad understood that Halloween night had definitely been a lesson learned the hard way.

Just then the doors of Reed's Hardware swung open. "What do you say we get that glove first and then go for some blueberry pancakes?" said Mr. Hawkins. Owen thought that was a great idea, the best he'd heard all morning.

He and his dad picked out the perfect glove. Owen could hardly wait to finish his pancakes and get home to try it out. It felt good to be excited about something again.

And wouldn't you know it — Todd was waiting on the front steps when Owen got home. In that instant all of Owen's worries seemed to fade away.

"Looks like you have a buddy to help you try out your new glove," Mr. Hawkins said, stopping the car. "Have a good time, son."

"Thanks, Dad . . . for everything."

"No problem, Owen. It's what I'm here for. Being your dad is the *best* job I have."

Wow, would you look at that ball fly!
I think Owen's going to fit in just fine here in Spencer's Mill.
Like every kid, he'll have some more tough choices to make
down the road. Sometimes it's hard to know what to do,
so just ask yourself what feels right.
Until we meet again, keep the twinkle in your eye,
the wind in your wings, and the goodness in your heart.

"So, what's it gonna be, Swamp Man, are you comin' or not?" Nick was getting impatient.

"Uh . . . sure," Owen said. He really wanted to fit in. And he knew he'd be mincemeat Monday morning at school if Nick and Eddie thought he was a chicken. Nobody would want to be friends with the kid who was the center of all the jokes.

Owen tried to act just like the other guys. He seemed to have everyone fooled, until one of the boys spotted their first target. "Hey, how 'bout those two goblin pumpkins?" he said, squatting behind a row of holly bushes.

The bushes looked familiar to Owen — way too familiar. They were his dad's holly bushes, and Amy's and Joey's pumpkins! He knew he had to say something fast.

"Uh . . . we can't smash those," he sputtered.

"Why not?" Eddie asked.

"'Cause it's my dad's house, and those are my little brother's and sister's pumpkins."

"Yeah, so?" Nick said, peeking over the bushes to get a better look.

"Well, I spent all afternoon carving those pumpkins. It was a lot of hard work. Can't we just skip this house?"

"Pretty good job, too," one of the boys said, admiring the pumpkins.

Nick finally gave the *Keep moving* signal. Owen let out a huge sigh of relief.

This wasn't going to be as easy as he'd thought. What if Amy and Joey had seen him? What would they think if they found out he'd gone pumpkin-smashing instead of trick-or-treating?

As the boys traveled up the street, they found plenty of pumpkins to smash, one right after another. Everyone seemed to love watching the jack-o'-lanterns explode when they hit the ground. Everyone except Owen, that is. When his turn came around, he kept giving it away to someone else.

Could Owen be thinking he made the wrong choice?
He had his doubts from the beginning, but did he listen to his instincts?

"Hey, Swamp Man, you haven't had a turn yet. How 'bout Ol' Man Drake's pumpkin?" Eddie said, pointing to the house at the next corner. A black iron fence wrapped around the front of the house and disappeared into a row of trees on the back side of the property. Usually when kids cut through Ol' Man Drake's yard, they hurdled the fence.

But Owen didn't need to worry about hurdling the fence, because Eddie was holding the gate wide open.

"Go ahead, it's all yours," whispered Nick.

"Uh, that's okay. Someone else can go." Owen held his breath, hoping one of the others would take his turn again. But instead they all started to chuckle.

"What do you know . . . he's chicken," one of the boys teased.

"Yeah, he's a sissy."

"What are you afraid of, Swamp Man?" Eddie asked.

The more they made fun of Owen, the louder they laughed. Owen wished they'd stop. He looked up at Ol' Man Drake's pumpkin, then back at the boys, and then at the pumpkin again. It definitely wasn't going to win any awards, Owen thought. Besides, maybe Ol' Man Drake would learn a lesson and start being nice if he got a dose of his own medicine. Owen knew if he didn't smash it, they'd all make fun of him for the rest of the year, and he could kiss his chances of making new friends good-bye.

"What are you waiting for, scaredy-cat?" Nick asked.

Owen couldn't take it anymore! *It's just a vegetable,* he told himself. *It's just a vegetable!* And with those words in his mind he ran up the walk, grabbed the small pumpkin, and threw it off the porch. The instant it left his fingertips, Owen wished he could get it back. He watched it tumble through the air and land face-first on the sidewalk. *Splat!*

"Way to go, Swamp Man!" Nick cheered. "Now, let's get out of here before Ol' Man Drake catches us!"

The boys scattered up the street and disappeared into the darkness. Owen walked back through the gate, pausing on the sidewalk to look down at the damage he had caused. It had been so easy, but now he felt awful. He just stood there not knowing what to do next. He didn't want to smash any more pumpkins, and if he caught up with Nick and Eddie, that's exactly what they'd expect him to do. But where else could he go? He spotted a group of kids crossing the street one block over.

If I can see them, thought Owen, *that means they can see me.* He realized they'd probably seen him smash Mr. Drake's pumpkin. Oh no! He recognized one of the costumes. It was Count Dracula. Owen looked away, hoping Todd hadn't recognized him.

"Wishful thinking," he said behind his mask. "I'm sooo caught in this costume!"

He knew he had to get out of there, and fast. If he went back to the gym, he'd have to face Todd and the other kids that had just seen him. He didn't want to catch up with Nick and Eddie, either; he'd had more than enough of them. There was only one place to go — his dad's! *He'll be home, and he can give me a ride back to the farm,* Owen thought. But he knew his dad would be surprised to see him, so he'd need to tell him something — but what?

Owen pushed the button next to the front door. He could hear the bell ring inside his dad's house. *I'll just tell him the truth,* he thought. *Things sure don't need to get any worse.*

Mr. Hawkins opened the door. "Son, what are you doing here? Is the party over already?"

"Not exactly," Owen said, looking up at his dad as he stepped inside. "Well, it's over for me, but not for everyone else." Owen sat down in the living room and began to explain, as best he could, everything that had happened.

"I only went so they wouldn't make fun of me. I knew if they thought I was chicken, I'd never be able to make friends at school. That's why I did it. That's why I smashed the pumpkin, and to make things worse, a fifth grader who lives down the road from the farm saw me do it."

"Okay, Owen, slow down, one thing at a time." Mr. Hawkins sat down on the sofa next to Owen. "First of all, I want you to know how proud I am of you. I know that coming here and telling me the truth wasn't easy. We're going to work through this together. It'll be okay, I promise."

Owen leaned back and tried to calm down.

"I don't know what I was thinkin'. I just didn't want them to make fun of me," he said.

Mr. Hawkins put his hand on Owen's knee. "You know, there will always be people who'll make fun of you, even when you're doing the right thing. They want to feel important, so they say things to try and make other people feel unimportant. It's their way of feeling in control — but they really aren't. Does that make sense, Owen?" Mr. Hawkins asked.

"I think so," said Owen. He was starting to feel a little better.

"We all make poor choices sometimes, and tonight was one of those times for you. But do you want to know the good news?" Mr. Hawkins asked.

"What do you mean?" Owen was confused. He wondered how *anything* good could have come out of the worst night of his life.

Mr. Hawkins explained, "Every time we make a mistake, we have a great opportunity to learn something. Now, let's see . . . you're sitting here feeling bad about the pumpkin you smashed, you're missing the party you were so excited about, and you're worried about this kid Todd and what he might be thinking. Is that about right?"

"I guess so," Owen answered. His dad had pretty much read his mind.

"And who do you think is to blame?" Mr. Hawkins asked, giving Owen a nudge.

"Me?"

"Bingo! The choices you made caused all of these things to happen. But the good news is . . . you can make things okay again."

"But how?" Owen wasn't convinced.

"I'll give you a few ideas, but then you have to figure it out on your own." Mr. Hawkins gave Owen a pat on the knee and then stood up. "You'll get it right, son. And you'll know when it's right, because you'll start to feel better about yourself." That couldn't come soon enough for Owen.

"Oh . . . one last thing," Mr. Hawkins said, looking down at Owen. "Do you know why Mr. Drake gets so upset when you kids cut through his yard? It's because he's been trying to get grass to grow for as long as I can remember. Every time you kids jump his fence, he has to put out more seed."

"No wonder he gets so upset," Owen said. He realized Mr. Drake wasn't just a grumpy old man after all. He actually had a good reason for not wanting kids in his yard.

"Now, how 'bout I give the school a call to let them know where you are, and then I'll call your mom to tell her you're spending the night with us?"

"That'd be great, Dad," Owen answered. He wanted to hear some of his dad's ideas before he went to bed. The sooner he got this mess worked out the better.

Owen woke up the next morning to a brand-new day, and he had a plan! He'd decided to talk to Todd and just explain what had happened. He knew if he didn't explain, Todd would think he was just like Nick and Eddie. But first he needed to apologize to Mr. Drake. He dreaded walking back through the iron gate and knocking on the front door. Just the thought of it made his heart pound inside his chest. Maybe he could offer to help Mr. Drake water his grass or put out more grass seed. Owen knew there was only one way to find out. He walked out the door, turned down the sidewalk, and headed toward Mr. Drake's house. He was ready to make things right!

I bet you know how Owen must be feeling.
But knowing he's doing the right thing gives him all the courage he needs.
He knows Nick and Eddie will probably give him a hard time at school,
but understanding why some kids tease other kids
will make it easier for Owen.

I'll tell you a secret . . .
Mr. Drake's been looking for a kid to work in his yard,
and Owen's perfect for the job. And there's something else —
Miss Hildy asked Todd to take Owen his prize.
That's right, Owen won the contest! And he'll have a chance
to explain everything to Todd when he gets back to the farm.

Have you learned something on this adventure?
Owen sure has. He'll probably remember this Halloween
for the rest of his life.

Well, it's time to be moving on.
Until we meet again, keep the twinkle in your eye,
the wind in your wings, and the goodness in your heart.

Questions for Thought

Beginning Questions:

How did Owen feel when he moved to Spencer's Mill?

How would you feel if your family told you that you were moving to another town and would be going to a new school?

Why did Owen think baseball would never be as much fun as lacrosse?

Why did Owen think Nick and Eddie were the coolest guys in his class?

How did Owen feel when he realized Nick and Eddie wanted to smash pumpkins?

Why did Nick and Eddie *want* Owen to smash pumpkins?

In Choice A:

If someone on the playground called you names, what names would hurt you most?

When Owen told Nick and Eddie he didn't think smashing pumpkins was a good idea, did anyone understand what Owen was saying? How could you tell?

How does it make you feel when someone leaves you out or calls you names?

Why is it important to choose your friends carefully?

Will Owen be a good role model for Amy and Joey?

In Choice B:

Why do you suppose Nick, Eddie, and the other boys ran off when they saw Todd and his friends, leaving Owen standing alone with the smashed pumpkin?

Why wasn't Owen excited about winning the contest?

What does "guilty by association" mean?

In Choice C:

Fitting in is important to many people. What are some of the positive and negative things people do to fit in?

Why didn't Owen just turn around and walk away when it was his turn to smash a pumpkin?

When did Owen show perseverance? Have you ever persevered in something that was hard to do?

Ending Questions:

Why was Owen so afraid Nick and Eddie would make fun of him?

When did Owen have a lot of courage?

What kind of reputation do you think Nick and Eddie had?

What is vandalism? Can you predict the consequences for Nick and Eddie's behavior?

What could you do to make a new student feel welcome?

Did the smashers want to be friends with Owen? Why or why not?

Why do you think Nick and Eddie treated people and acted the way they did?

What is your conscience? What did Owen's conscience make him do?

Without mentioning names, have you ever known anyone like Nick and Eddie?

Have you ever made a choice that you wish you hadn't made? What did you learn?

What do Owen's decisions tell you about his character?

Have you ever known anyone like Todd? Do you think Todd will be a good friend? Why?

ABOUT THE AUTHORS

*Leah Butler,
age 5 in 1970*

*Trudy Peters,
age 5 in 1954*

Leah Butler and Trudy Peters met in 1989 while publishing a magazine in Nashville, Tennessee. They quickly realized their shared philosophies and zest for life made them a strong team.

Although careers and life choices have landed them in different geographic locations, their solid friendship has spanned the distance. When the two of them come together, the atmosphere is charged with creativity and camaraderie.

Leah lives in Charlotte, North Carolina, with her husband and three children.

Trudy lives outside Nashville in an 1832 log home with four furry "best friends."

ABOUT THE ILLUSTRATOR

*Neal Armstrong,
age 6 in 1977*

Neal Armstrong was born in Atikokan, Ontario, Canada. Influenced by the great classical painters of the past, Neal continues the tradition of highly rendered oil paintings, and his artwork has garnered him many international awards. Neal's passion is creating illustrations that invite the viewer into a world of fantasy and adventure. He currently lives in Longueuil, Quebec, with his wife, Dominique, and their daughter, Lucie.